From all your friends in the garden
Best Wishes & Happy Reading
Lenore Masterson

Leapin', Lizards!
Bebe and Poppy are at it again!
Enjoy the adventure!
Kathleen Ambro

Dedicated

To my husband, John, you are the wind beneath my wings.
To my granddaughter, Emma who is ever so huggable.
K.A.

To Howard and Bev Sherman who saw my destiny long before I even had the dream.
Thank you!
L.M.

Positive Waves Publishing

Text and illustrations copyright © 2009 by Kathleen Ambro
Written by Kathleen Ambro; Illustrated by Lenore Masterson

Library of Congress Cataloging-in-Publication Data
Ambro, Kathleen. The Adventures of Bebe and Poppy – Horrible Horrace.

First edition published 2009 by Positive Waves Publishing:
Positive Waves Publishing
225 Crossroads Blvd. Suite 332
Carmel, CA 93923

Library of Congress Control Number: 2009909461

ISBN: 978-0-578-03832-2

1. Lizards – Juvenile fiction. 2. Tennis shoes – Juvenile fiction. 3. Garden – Juvenile fiction.
4. Dealing with a bully – Juvenile fiction.

Signature Book Printing, Inc
www.sbpbooks.com
First printing, September 2009
Printed in the United States of America

The Adventures of Bebe and Poppy

Horrible Horrace

Written by Kathleen Ambro
Illustrated by Lenore Masterson

"What's that noise?" asked Poppy, awakened from a sound sleep.

!!Screech!!
!! Slam!!
!!Bang!!

Bebe crawled from under a bush and peeked out. "It's a moving van. We're getting new neighbors."

"I hope they don't have a cat." Poppy yawned. "Well, come on, Bebe, let's go take a look."

As they raced through the garden,
Poppy stumbled and landed in a mud puddle.
SPLASH!
"Oh, I'm so sorry," said a deep voice.
They looked around,
but couldn't see anyone.
"Please forgive me?" said the voice.

"Where are you?" asked Poppy.

"I'm over here."

Poppy looked back, but only saw what looked like a rock.
Slowly it began to move. "It's Tully the turtle," said Bebe.
"You really ought to pick a better place to sleep."

"So, you're the one
who tripped me!" yelled Poppy
shaking the mud from his shirt.

Tully's eyes closed. He began to snore.
"Wake up!" yelled Bebe, shaking Tully's shell.
"Don't sleep now. We have new neighbors to meet."

Tully opened one eye. "You go ahead.
I'm feeling a bit sluggish today."
"I'll carry you," said Poppy.
"I don't know . . ." said Tully.
"It's okay," said Poppy.
"Bebe will boost you onto my back."

"No problem," said Bebe. "I'll give you a push . . ."

Bebe pushed so hard that Tully flipped over Poppy's head, landing on a rusty skate.
"Help!" yelled Tully, clinging to the skate. It zoomed off the garden path . . .
   SMACK
   . . . into a stone wall, shooting Tully high above the trees.

"Oh, dear," said Bebe, "I can't watch."

He covered his eyes waiting for Tully to land . . .
   SPLAT
   . . . on the ground, but there was no sound.

"The view is much better up here,"
called a voice high above them.
Bebe and Poppy looked up.

There was Tully caught in a tree branch.
"Tully, are you all right?" they asked.
"I will be, as soon as you GET ME OUT OF THIS TREE!"
shouted Tully.

Squirrels scampered up the tree and pulled the branch
down low. Just as Bebe and Poppy reached out and
caught Tully, the ground shook.

"What was that?" Bebe asked.

Rapid Moving →

"Oh dear! Oh my!" cried Simon the snail, shivering in his shell.
A scaly gray and black blob tumbled from the moving van.
"It's a DINOSAUR!"

"No it's not," said Poppy with a big smile. "It's another lizard."
"He looks HUGE for a lizard," said Simon.
"Come on, let's go meet him," said Bebe.

"You lead the way," shouted the other animals.
So Bebe and Poppy led them across the street,
first looking left, then right, then left again.

The big lizard had his back toward them, and as he turned, swatted the animals with his heavy tail.
"Hey, what's the big idea?" asked Poppy.
"We came to welcome you to our neighborhood."

The monstrous lizard glared at them.
"Your neighborhood!" he shouted. "This is MY neighborhood now! And the name is Horrace! Capital H-O-R-R-A-C-E, HORRACE! And DON'T FORGET IT!" He stomped off, the ground shaking with each step.

"He's horrible!" yelled Bebe.

The grasshoppers sang out, "Horrible Horrace, he's no fun, send him back where he came from!"

One by one the animals returned to their homes in the garden, wondering what Horrible Horrace would do to their neighborhood.

That afternoon, Bebe and Poppy were busy at their shop, when suddenly the ground shook. Frightened customers ran from the shop. Bebe and Poppy stayed behind to keep the shelves of shoes from falling. Finally the ground stopped shaking.

"Whew!" sighed Bebe, putting a pair of shoes back on the shelf. "I d-d-d-don't like earthquakes."

"Ha, Ha, Ha! I'm your earthquake," said Horrible Horrace laughing as he plowed his way through the door. "Even the ground trembles when I'm around. Say, what are those funny looking things on the shelves?" he asked.
"They're tennis shoes, can't you read?" snapped Bebe.
"This is Bebe and Poppy's Tennis Shoe Shop!"

"But, lizards don't wear tennis shoes," said Horrace.
"They do now," said Poppy. "With tennis shoes, we can
outrun any old cats."
"Okay, give me a pair," demanded Horrace.
"Right this way," said Poppy. Have a seat on this bench.
Bebe brought over several boxes of shoes, but none of the
shoes fit Horrace's big feet.

      Horrace jumped up clutching his fists,
then swung his tail, knocking down all the tennis shoes.
He snooped around the shop, then turned to Poppy.
"This would make a great house."

Bebe sat down and started to cry.
"Oh dear, we're doomed!" he said
putting his head in his hands.

"We're not doomed," said Poppy. "It's just a minor set-back,
that's all. Now help me clean up this mess."
"Why bother," Bebe said. "Horrible Horrace will be moving
in tomorrow."
"Oh, no he won't," said Poppy. "We're not going to let him."

"I get it." Bebe smiled
and jumped to his feet.
"We're going to fight him.
Just let me at him.
First I'll trip him with shoelaces.
Then you can tie his feet together
and we'll push him out the door.
We'll show him who's boss."

Poppy rolled with laughter.

"I can just see that. The first time the ground
shakes, you'll be shivering under a bush."
"I suppose you have a better idea," said Bebe
as he helped Poppy pick up the scattered shoes.
"I sure do," said Poppy. "I've got a plan . . ."

That night when all the other animals were asleep, Bebe and Poppy were hard at work in their shop. Poppy cut out shapes, Bebe sewed, and they both glued on the rubber soles.

It was early the next morning when Poppy placed the new tennis shoes on a shelf behind the counter. With droopy eyelids, Bebe hung the "Open for Business" sign in the window. Luckily business was slow, so they took turns napping.

"What if this doesn't work?" asked Bebe.
"He's going to be awfully mad."
"Don't worry, I'll do the talking." said Poppy.
Suddenly the door flew open. In stomped Horrace.
"Why are those tennis shoes still here?" he yelled.
"Good afternoon, Horrace," said Poppy.
He dusted off a bench, "Please sit down.
We have a surprise for you."

"A surprise for me?" asked Horrace,
draping his tail over the bench as he sat down.

Poppy reached behind the counter and retrieved
an enormous pair of black and yellow tennis shoes.
"These ought to fit you just right," said Poppy.
Your new **THUNDERBOLT** tennis shoes!

Poppy pushed and tugged Horrace's feet,
until they slid into the shoes.
A huge tear rolled down Horrace's face.
"Oh dear!" shouted Poppy.
"Quick, Bebe, help me get these shoes off."
Bebe ran to help Poppy.

"No! Don't take them off," sniffled Horrace.
"They fit perfectly."
"Then why are you crying?" asked Bebe.

"Nobody has ever been kind to me. Everyone teases me because of my size. I have no friends. Everyone hides from me." Horrace sighed.

"We'll be your friends," said Poppy. "We've made something extra special for you." Bebe pushed out a large box filled with tennis shoes in a rainbow of colors, all for Horrace.

"I don't know what to say." Horrace smiled. "They're so beautiful!"

"Just be our friend," said Poppy.

"I'll do better than that. I'll protect your Tennis Shoe Shop and the garden from any mean old cats."

The next day, Horrace was excited to show off his new shoes.
He walked through the garden, but saw no other animals.
At the Tennis Shoe Shop, Bebe and Poppy were nowhere
to be found.

Oh, no, thought Horrace. Did I frighten everyone away?
Then Horrace heard a commotion at the far end of the
garden and ran to see what was going on.

When he pushed back the bushes, he heard . . .

He saw a table piled high with food and a banner that read:
"In Honor of Horrace, Our Protector and Friend."

Horrace was so happy he hugged everyone in sight,
and from then on was known as HUGGABLE HORRACE.

Parents and Teachers: *The Adventures of Bebe and Poppy* is a series written to encourage good character traits in children using the comical lizards, Bebe and Poppy.

In the first book, *Why Lizards Wear Tennis Shoes* children are introduced to both good and bad character traits woven throughout the story to teach children that making wise choices can affect their lives in a positive way.

In the second book, *Horrible Horrace* Bebe and Poppy take a bad situation and turn it into something good when a bully who has moved into their neighborhood wants to take over their tennis shoe shop.

I hope you enjoyed Bebe and Poppy in their adventures as they worked together to solve a very BIG problem with a bully in *Horrible Horrace*.

~Kathleen Ambro~
www.kathleenambro.com